C901921937

LIBRARIES NI
WITHDRAWN FROM STOCK

Dedicated to Marilyn Malin, for
putting up with us for so long.

This Faber book belongs to

...............................................................................

First published in the UK in 2016
by Faber and Faber Ltd,
Bloomsbury House,
74-77 Great Russell Street, London WC1B 3DA

Printed in Malta by Gutenberg Press Ltd.

All rights reserved

Text copyright © Diane Fox and illustrations copyright © Christyan Fox 2016

The rights of Diane and Christyan Fox to be identified as the author and illustrator of this work have
been asserted by them in accordance with the Copyright, Designs and Patent Act, 1988 (United Kingdom).

Endpaper image used with kind permission of CommentNation.com

A CIP record for this book is available
from the British Library

ISBN 978-0-571-32943-4 hardback

ISBN 978-0-571-32944-1 paperback

2 4 6 8 10 9 7 5 3 1

# A Dog Called Bear

## Diane and Christyan Fox

ff

FABER & FABER

Lucy had always wanted a dog.

She'd read all the doggie books.
She'd collected doggie pictures from magazines.
She'd saved all her money to buy doggie things.

One day Lucy set off in search
of a dog of her own . . .

Hello, my name is Lucy
and I'm looking for a dog.

I have a very nice basket at home,
and if I had a dog I would
love him and care for him and
take him for walks every day.

But dogs are licky and barky
and smelly. I would make a
much better pet, as long as
I can have a bath every day.

Oh, that's a pity,
I only have a shower.
Otherwise, I might have
been very tempted.

Soon Lucy met another animal.

Excuse me, I'm looking for a dog.

I have all the food he could eat, and I would love him and care for him and take him for walks every day.

I'm very similar to a dog but I'm not very keen on living indoors. Could we try it for three days a week?

Well, I was really looking for a full-time dog, but I can put your name on the list and if nothing else comes along I'll let you know.

Excuse me, I'm sorry to bother you, but I'm a lost dog who's looking for a nice basket in a home with lots of food, a garden to play in, and someone to love me and care for me and take me for walks every day.

What a lucky coincidence!

But are you absolutely sure you're a dog? I can't see any like you in my book.

Oh, that must be
an old book. Lots of
new dogs have been
invented recently.

My name's Bear.

That's a funny
name for a dog.

But, it's getting
late so I suppose
you'll have to do.

Bear settled in well.
The basket was
a bit small . . .

but the food was
very tasty . . .

the garden was very large . . .

the books were very informative . . .

the doggie
toys were fun . . .

and Lucy loved
and cared for him.

But one day Bear went to sleep.
And he slept through November, December,
January, February and March.

Which might not have been so bad
if he hadn't taken all the covers
*and* all the space in Lucy's bed.

In fact, being a dog owner was more
difficult than Lucy had thought . . .

I can't **STAND** the mess!

I can't **STAND** the digging!

I can't **STAND** the endless
bowls of porridge!

Being a pet dog wasn't easy, either . . .

Well, I'm fed up with having to carry YOUR sticks all the time.

And every time I bring YOUR ball back, YOU throw it away again!

And whenever I try to have a nap, YOU keep waking me up!

One day Bear was so cross, he decided to run away.

Dear Lucy,

Goodbye
FOREVER!

Bear

But after a day and a night Bear
missed his basket and his toys.

He missed his garden and he was hungry.
But most of all he missed Lucy.

Bear realised he was lonely
and had nowhere to go.

A piece of paper blew along the ground . . .

# MORE FABER PICTURE BOOKS . . .

Growing up
with Faber
www.faber.co.uk